W9-DJL-824

Boots Visits Grandma

Written by
Sara James

Illustrated by
Pamiel Barcita

SMITHMARK

Copyright © 1993 Kidsbooks Inc.

Kidsbooks Inc.
7004 N. California Avenue
Chicago, IL 60645

This edition published in 1993 by SMITHMARK Publishers Inc.,
16 East 32nd Street, New York, NY 10016.

All rights reserved including the right
of reproduction in whole or in part in any form.

SMITHMARK books are available for bulk purchase
for sales promotion and premium use.
For details, write or telephone the Manager of Special Sales,
SMITHMARK Publishers Inc., 16 East 32nd Street,
New York, NY 10016. (212) 532-6600

Manufactured in the United States of America

"Are you ready, son?" asked Dad.
"I'm coming," called Boots.

Boots was picking a big bunch
of daisies for someone very special. He picked his
last flower and then grabbed his skateboard from
the side of the house.

"See you later Dad,"
said Boots.
"You have a good time with
Grandma today," said Dad.

Boots loved surprising Grandma with a visit. She always had such fun things for him to do no matter when he stopped by.

When Boots reached Grandma's house he parked his skateboard outside and knocked on the door.

"Who is it?" asked Grandma.

"Surprise special delivery," answered Boots.

When Grandma opened the door, Boots handed her the flowers. "They're the special delivery and I'm the surprise," he said.

"What a wonderful surprise you are," said Grandma as she scooped Boots into her arms.

As they walked inside, the sweet smell of freshly baked cookies filled the air.

"I smell chocolate chip cookies," said Boots. "Can I have one now, please, please?" he begged.

"First let's have some lunch," said Grandma.

After a hearty lunch, and five delicious cookies for dessert, Boots was ready for something fun to do.

"What are we going to do today?" he asked.

"I thought we might look at one of my old photo albums," said Grandma. "Would you like that?"

"That sounds super," answered Boots.

Boots climbed up on Grandma's big comfortable sofa while she went to get the album.

"Wow, you look so pretty in this picture," said Boots as he turned to the first page.

"And Grandpa looks so handsome."

"Hey, is that me?" asked Boots as he pointed to the next picture.

"No. That's your grandfather when he was just about your age," said Grandma.

"But he looks just like me," said Boots. "He has white paws like I do and the same orange and brown stripes, too."

"You inherited them from him," said Grandma.

"In..her..ited. What's that mean?" asked Boots.
"It means you received special traits that were passe
down through the family," explained Grandma.

"You mean Grandpa passed down his looks to me," said Boots.

"Exactly," agreed Grandma.

"Boy, am I lucky," said Boots. "He sure was handsome."

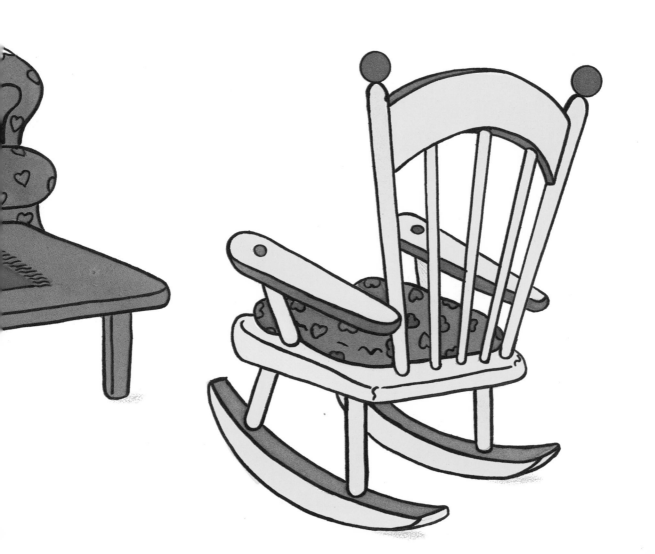

On the next page was a picture of Grandma as a little kitten. She was eating an ice-cream cone.

"That looks delicious," said Boots. "Ice cream is one of my favorites."

"Mine, too," said Grandma.

"I guess I inherited my love of ice cream from you," giggled Boots.

"Who is that?" asked Boots as he turned the page.

"That's your father. In this picture he's just a tiny little kitten," said Grandma.

"Except for the same color eyes, how come I don't look very much like him?" asked Boots.

"Well," said Grandma, "that's because your dad looks more like my side of the family."

Just then there was a knock at the door.

"Who is it?" shouted Boots.

"It's Daddy," said his father.

"How are my favorite son and mom doing?" he asked.

"Well, we looked at the photo album, and do you know that I look just like Grandpa?" asked Boots.

"But you and I have the same color eyes."

"And I bet you discovered that you and Grandma love ice cream, too," said Dad.

"You bet we do," said Boots.

Just then Dad handed Boots the carton of ice cream he had been hiding behind his back, and Grandma hurried to get the cones.